A. A. MILNE

Christopher Robin
Gives Pooh a Party

illustrated by

E. H. SHEPARD

DUTTON CHILDREN'S BOOKS

Christopher Robin Gives Pooh a Party

*It had rained and rained so that
the tree that was Piglet's home
was entirely surrounded by water.
He was rescued by Pooh, who set
out first on a honey jar (which
he named* The Floating Bear*) and
then in Christopher Robin's
umbrella (which he named*
The Brain of Pooh*).*

One day when the sun had come back
over the Forest, bringing with it the scent
of may, and all the streams of the
Forest were tinkling happily to find
themselves their own pretty shape again,

and the little pools lay dreaming of the life they had seen and the big things they had done, and in the warmth and quiet of the Forest the cuckoo was trying over his voice carefully and listening to see if he liked it, and wood-pigeons were complaining gently to themselves in their lazy comfortable way that it was the other fellow's fault, but it didn't matter very much; on such a day as this Christopher Robin whistled in a special way he had, and Owl came flying out of the Hundred Acre Wood to see what was wanted.

'Owl,' said Christopher Robin, 'I am going to give a party.'

'You are, are you?' said Owl.

'And it's to be a special sort of party, because it's because of what Pooh did when he did what he did to save Piglet from the flood.'

'Oh, that's what it's for, is it?' said Owl.

'Yes, so will you tell Pooh as quickly

as you can, and all the others, because it
will be to-morrow?'

'Oh, it will, will it?' said Owl, still
being as helpful as possible.

'So will you go and tell them, Owl?'

Owl tried to think of something very
wise to say, but couldn't, so he flew off
to tell the others. And the first person
he told was Pooh.

'Pooh,' he said, 'Christopher Robin
is giving a party.'

'Oh!' said Pooh. And then seeing that Owl
expected him to say something else,
he said, 'Will there be those little cake things
with pink sugar icing?'

Owl felt that it was rather beneath him
to talk about little cake things
with pink sugar icing, so he told Pooh
exactly what Christopher Robin had said,
and flew off to Eeyore.

'A party for me?' thought Pooh to himself.
'How grand!' And he began

to wonder if all the other animals
would know that it was a special
Pooh party, and if Christopher Robin
had told them about *The Floating
Bear* and the *Brain of Pooh* and all

the wonderful ships he had invented
and sailed on, and he began to think
how awful it would be if everybody
had forgotten about it, and nobody
quite knew what the party was for;
and the more he thought like this,

the more the party got muddled in
his mind, like a dream when nothing
goes right. And the dream began to
sing itself over in his head until it
became a sort of song. It was an

ANXIOUS POOH SONG

3 Cheers for Pooh!
(For Who?)
For Pooh –
(Why what did he do?)
I thought you knew;
He saved his friend from a wetting!
3 Cheers for Bear!
(For where?)
For Bear –
He couldn't swim,
But he rescued him!
(He rescued who?)
Oh, listen, do!
I am talking of Pooh –
(Of who?)
Of Pooh!
(I'm sorry I keep forgetting.)

Well, Pooh was a Bear of Enormous Brain –
(Just say it again!)
Of enormous brain –
(Of enormous what?)
Well, he ate a lot,
And I don't know if he could swim or not,
But he managed to float
On a sort of boat
(On a sort of what?)
Well, a sort of pot –
So now let's give him three hearty cheers
(So now let's give him three hearty whiches!)
And hope he'll be with us for years and years,

And grow in health and wisdom and riches!
3 Cheers for Pooh!
(For who?)
For Pooh –
3 Cheers for Bear!
(For where?)
For Bear –

While this was going on inside him,
Owl was talking to Eeyore.

'Eeyore,' said Owl, 'Christopher Robin
is giving a party.'

'Very interesting,' said Eeyore.

'I suppose they will be sending me down
the odd bits which got trodden on. Kind and
thoughtful. Not at all, don't mention it.'

'There is an Invitation for you.'

'What's that like?'

'An Invitation!'

'Yes, I heard you. Who dropped it?'

'This isn't anything to eat, it's asking you to the party. To-morrow.'

Eeyore shook his head slowly.

'You mean Piglet. The little fellow with the excited ears. That's Piglet. I'll tell him.'

'No, no!' said Owl, getting quite fussy. 'It's you!'

'Are you sure?'

'Of course I'm sure. Christopher

Robin said "All of them! Tell all of them".'

'All of them, except Eeyore?'

'All of them,' said Owl sulkily.

'Ah!' said Eeyore. 'A mistake, no doubt, but still, I shall come. Only don't blame *me* if it rains.'

But it didn't rain. Christopher Robin had made a long table out of some long pieces of wood, and they all sat round it.

Christopher Robin sat at one end, and
Pooh sat at the other, and between them
on one side were Owl and Eeyore and Piglet,

and between them on the other side were
Rabbit, and Roo and Kanga. And all Rabbit's
friends and relations spread themselves
about on the grass, and waited hopefully
in case anybody spoke to them, or
dropped anything, or asked them the time.

It was the first party to which Roo had
ever been, and he was very excited. As soon

as ever they had sat down he began to talk.

'Hallo, Pooh!' he squeaked.

'Hallo, Roo!' said Pooh.

Roo jumped up and down in his seat for a little while and then began again.

'Hallo, Piglet!' he squeaked.

Piglet waved a paw at him, being too busy to say anything.

'Hallo, Eeyore!' said Roo.

Eeyore nodded gloomily at him. 'It will rain soon, you see if it doesn't,' he said.

Roo looked to see if it didn't, and it didn't, so he said 'Hallo, Owl!' and Owl said 'Hallo, my little fellow,' in a kindly way, and went on telling Christopher Robin about an accident which had nearly happened to a friend of his whom Christopher Robin didn't know, and Kanga said to Roo, 'Drink up your milk first, dear, and talk afterwards.' So Roo, who was drinking his milk, tried to say that he could do both at once . . . and had to be patted on the back and dried for quite a long time afterwards.

When they had all nearly eaten enough, Christopher Robin banged on the table with his spoon, and everybody stopped talking and was very silent, except Roo who was just finishing a loud attack of hiccups and trying to look as if it was one of Rabbit's relations.

'This party,' said Christopher Robin, 'is a party because of what someone did, and we all know who it was, and it's his party, because of what he did, and I've got a present for him and here it is.' Then he felt about a little and whispered, 'Where is it?'

While he was looking Eeyore coughed in an impressive way and began to speak.

'Friends,' he said, 'including oddments, it is a great pleasure, or perhaps I had better say it has been a pleasure so far, to see you at my party. What I did

was nothing. Any of you – except Rabbit
and Owl and Kanga – would have done the
same. Oh, and Pooh. My remarks do not,

of course, apply to Piglet and Roo,
because they are too small. Any of you
would have done the same. But it just

happened to be Me. It was not, I need hardly say, with an idea of getting what Christopher Robin is looking for now' – and he put his front leg to his mouth and said in a loud whisper, 'Try under the table' – 'that I did what I did – but because I feel that we should all do what we can to help. I feel that we should all—'

'H – hup!' said Roo accidentally.

'Roo, dear!' said Kanga reproachfully.

'Was it me?' asked Roo, a little surprised.

'What's Eeyore talking about?' Piglet whispered to Pooh.

'I don't know,' said Pooh rather dolefully.

'I thought this was *your* party.'

'I thought it was *once*. But I suppose it isn't.'

'I'd sooner it was yours than Eeyore's,' said Piglet.

'So would I,' said Pooh.

'H – hup!' said Roo again.

'AS – I – WAS – SAYING,' said Eeyore loudly and sternly, 'as I was saying when I was interrupted by various Loud Sounds, I feel that—'

'Here it is!' cried Christopher Robin excitely. 'Pass it down to silly old Pooh. It's for Pooh.'

'For Pooh?' said Eeyore.

'Of course it is. The best bear in all the world.'

'I might have known,' said Eeyore. 'After all, one can't complain. I have my friends. Somebody spoke to me only yesterday. And was it last week or the week before that Rabbit bumped into me and said "Bother!" The Social Round. Always something going on.'

Nobody was listening, for they were all saying, 'Open it, Pooh.' 'What is it, Pooh?' 'I know what it is,' 'No, you don't,' and other helpful remarks of this sort. And of course Pooh was opening it as quickly as ever he could, but without cutting the string, because you never know when a bit of string might be Useful. At last it was undone.

When Pooh saw what it was, he nearly fell down, he was so pleased. It was a

Special Pencil Case. There were pencils in it marked 'B' for Bear, and pencils marked 'HB' for Helping Bear, and pencils marked

'BB' for Brave Bear. There was a knife for sharpening the pencils, an india-rubber for rubbing out anything which you

had spelt wrong, and a ruler for ruling
lines for the words to walk on, and
inches marked on the ruler in case you
wanted to know how many inches anything
was, and Blue Pencils and Red Pencils
and Green Pencils for saying special
things in blue and red and green. And
all these lovely things were in little
pockets of their own in a Special Case
which shut with a click when you clicked
it. And they were all for Pooh.

'Oh!' said Pooh.

'Oh, Pooh!' said everybody else
except Eeyore.

'Thank you,' growled Pooh.

But Eeyore was saying to himself,
'This writing business.
Pencils and
what-not. Over-rated,
if you ask me.
Silly stuff. Nothing
in it.'

Pooh

Later on, when they had all said 'Good-
bye' and 'Thank-you' to Christopher Robin,

Pooh and Piglet walked home thoughtfully
together in the golden evening, and for a
long time they were silent.

'When you wake up in the morning, Pooh,'
said Piglet at last, 'what's the first thing
you say to yourself?'

'What's for breakfast?' said Pooh.
'What do *you* say, Piglet?'

'I say, I wonder what's going to happen
exciting *today*?' said Piglet.

Pooh nodded thoughtfully.

'It's the same thing,' he said.